# Neighborly Pleasures

When my electric push lawn mower died from cutting too big of a lawn, I decided to splurge and get a fancy new electric riding lawn mower, the Pro 60V" crossoverz zero turn Lawn mower that comes with 6 batteries.

Anyways I was finishing up my lush lawn when I saw my neighbors Steve, Sarah and their daughter Shelby with suitcases loading up their new Toyota tundra.

I went over to them and said how come you guys didn't tell me that you're going on a trip, I'll miss you guys. Sarah said we are not going on a trip our fucking Air conditioning just crapped out.

I said oh no and its 100 degrees today wow. I said so when can they fix it. Steve said not for two weeks. I said those motherfuckers. Shelby said tell me about it, I just came home from college and this shit happens.

I said so where are you guys going. Steve said we are going to a hotel until we can get the air conditioning fixed. I said the hell you are; you guys are staying with me.

I can't have my favorite neighbors staying at a fucking hotel. Sarah said we don't want to bother you. I said it's not a bother, now get your asses inside my house before we burn to death in this fucking heat.

Shelby said I'm going to the generous neighbor's house; I don't know about you guys. Steve turned off the truck and I helped them bring all their stuff into my house.

I showed them to the guest bedrooms, and we offloaded their stuff. I showed them my bedroom, where the pool was, I showed Steve my man cave. He said oh my god I'm never leaving. I showed Steve the fridge with cold Bud light and Sarah my wine collection that was fully stocked.

I told them when you finish something, write it on this sticky note and I'll replace it. I said all rooms are a panic rooms so if anything happens stay here and close the door. I showed them my gun safe just in case shit pops off. I opened it and Shelby said holy shit dad, his gun safe is fully stocked. Sarah said oh yeah safety smiling at me.

I showed them my home office. I gave them the codes to the stuff they needed to put in their phones because there are too many numbers to remember. I said last but not least I took them to my movie theatre.

Shelby said this is way better than a hotel. I smiled at her and Sarah said thanks for inviting us to stay. I said my pleasure and you make the best spaghetti, Sarah. I took them to my chef's kitchen.

Sarah said oh my god this is heaven, I could stay in here all day. I showed her the fully stocked subzero refrigerator built into the wall. Steve said my god, I had no idea all of this shit was in here.

I said Steve, do you want to see the gun range out back below the swimming pool. Steve said oh hell yeah, we all went out back and into the ground beneath the pool.

I showed them all how to use it and that there was a second gun safe fully stocked for the gun range. I said now you know it all. Steve said wow this is incredible then he said I'll be in the man cave watching sports on the giant projector.

Sarah said I'll be in the kitchen cooking something and relaxing. Shelby said I'll be at the pool and talking to my friends on my cell phone. I said I'll be taking a nap in my bedroom, if you guys need me, you know where to find me.

We left the underground bunker and went in all different directions. I went to take a nap. Later, Sarah came to my bedroom, she rubbed my chest and said dinner is ready honey.

I woke up and smelt it, Sarah said I made your favorite spaghetti. I said Sarah, you are the best. She smiled and said I know. We went downstairs, Steve and Shelby said we are ready to eat.

We all sat and ate until we couldn't eat anymore. I said that was amazing Sarah thank you so much, I should keep you guys here forever. Shelby said you wouldn't get any resistance from me. Sarah said I love your kitchen; I'd love to stay here forever. Steve said I love your man cave; I could stay there forever.

I said I am glad to hear my favorite neighbors are happy and relaxed. Shelby said thank you so much for letting us stay in your lovely home with a pool. I said you're welcome, Shelby.

Steve and Sarah said we can't thank you enough for the hospitality. I said your cooking is all the thanks that I need looking at hot Sarah. She said you're welcome honey and hugged me tight with her perfect body. Shelby said can I hug you too. I said sure, she hugged me with her perfect body given to her by her hot mom.

Steve said I'm not a hugger, but he shook my hand and patted me on my shoulders saying thank you. I said you guys relax, I'll be in my room. I left them to their own devices.

I went to my room; I was watching television and it was too quiet. So, I turned on my monitors on my laptop to see what each of them were up to. Shelby was on her bed in her bra and panties talking to her friends on the phone.

I looked at the camera for my man cave. Steve was fucking Sarah doggie bent over the couch. I thought damn that's fucking hot. I rewind from the beginning. Sarah first started sucking Steve's cock on her knees then he ate her pussy as she laid on the couch.

Steve mounted her missionary style as she creamed his cock then they switch to doggie where he pulled her hair and fucked her hard. I thought damn Sarah loves her cock and I love 4k cameras. It was so hot watching Sarah get fucked, with her big tits bouncing and juicy big ass jiggling until Steve ejaculated inside of his hot wife.

They hugged and kissed while cuddling for a while then they went up to their guest bedroom. Shelby was getting ready for bed moisturizing her hot naked body and then went to bed totally naked. I went to sleep after that, I woke up Sunday when Sarah came to my bedroom in a very revealing nightgown. She said breakfast is ready, I said good morning, Sarah.

Sarah said good morning and gave me a peck on the lips. I thought nothing of it, and we went down to breakfast. Steve was there in pajamas and Shelby was wearing a big t-shirt I'm sure nothing was under it.

We sat and ate breakfast like we were family. Steve said can you give me a ride to the airport buddy. I said sure, how long are you gone for, and he said two weeks, so take care of my girls for me. I said sure no problem, I'll keep your girls safe.

Hours later, Steve was all packed and ready to go. We loaded up my Toyota Tundra and went to the airport. A long the way, Steve said thanks, you saved us from having to go to a hotel and spend a shit load of money for two weeks. I said happy to help out my favorite neighbors. Your wife is a great cook, I love all the food she makes.

Steve said one of many reasons that I married her. I said you are both lucky to have each other and you have a wonderful daughter Shelby who is a fish. She is in a pool all the time.

Steve said she loves swimming, and we don't have a pool so there you go. I said she can still come over and swim when you get your Air conditioner fixed. Steve said be sure and tell her that when you get back. I said I will, Steve said do you mind if I hang in your man cave when we get our air conditioning back.

I said you are welcome anytime. Steve said sweet, Sarah drank a bottle of wine last night and wrote it on the sticky note. I said good girl, I said how are the beers doing. Steve said I finished a six pack and I put it on a sticky note. I said good man.

We reached the airport and I dropped Steve at the terminal. We hugged goodbye and he was on his way. I went back home to Sarah and Shelby. Sarah was in the kitchen when I came back baking something that smelt really good. She hugged and kissed me on the lips when she saw me.

I said I need to tell Shelby that she can use the pool when you get your air conditioning fixed. Sarah said she will love that a lot, my little girl is a fish, she loves the water.

I said she is 6 foot tall like both of us, she is not that little. Sarah said yeah, I know but she will always be my little girl. I said I understand. I went out to talk to Shelby at the pool.

I told her that she could use the pool when they get their air conditioning fixed. Shelby jumped up and down jiggling her amazing goodies. She hugged me and gave me a peck on the lips. I smiled at her then she said would you mind rubbing some sunscreen on me. I said sure no problem.

I rubbed sunscreen all over Shelby's hot body wow, which was a treat and a half, then I went back inside. Sarah hugged me tight and said that was very sweet of you to let her use your pool. She kissed me on the lips again then said can I use your pool too. I said sure Sarah, you and Steve may use my pool too, you have the codes in your phone already.

Sarah said cool, you are the best, hugging me with her hot body and kissing me again.

Sarah looked amazing in her short summer dress, which showed off her amazing ass when she walked around the kitchen and her big titties were popping out of her vest that showed amazing cleavage.

Later that Sunday night, when it was time for bed. Shelby hugged and kissed me goodnight. Sarah hugged and kissed me goodnight too. I went up to my bedroom and prepared for sleep. I heard a knock on the door, I used my remote to open the door, it was Sarah in a very revealing red lingerie.

I thought wow, she said can I sleep in your bed tonight, I hate sleeping alone when Steve is gone. I said sure there is plenty of room in this California split king sleep number bed.

Sarah climbed into my bed then snuggled up to me as we watched the news. The weatherman told us that it was going to be hot for the next two weeks, triple digits every day. Sarah said wow, our air conditioning broke at the right time. We both laughed out loud.

Sarah kissed me again this time I held her and kissed her back. When we came up for air, Sarah kissed down my chest to my abs. She took my boxers off then engulfed my black cock with her wonderful mouth, damn Sarah really knew how to suck a mean dick wow.

She sucked my black cock for a little bit then slid down my black cock with her tight white pussy. I squeezed her big fucking tits as she fucked my cock up and down. Damn it felt amazing to be in Sarah after desiring her for years as my neighbor.

Sarah moaned and said I'm cumming all over your big black cock baby, it feels so good inside my white vagina. She said do you like my white vagina moisturizing your big black cock. I said oh yeah Sarah, she said I've wanted your black cock in me for years now. I said I've wanted your white pussy for years too.

Sarah said do you want to bend me over, smack my fat ass, pull my fucking hair and fuck me until you ejaculate inside of my white pussy.

I said yes please, Sarah flashed me a smile on her pretty face. She bent over and I smacked her fat ass. I slammed my cock up her cunt and pulled her fucking hair.

I went to town on her white pussy. I gave her a proper roman fucking. Sarah said oh god I love getting pounded by your big fucking cock.

I couldn't handle the pressure anymore, so I let my pleasure valve go releasing a torrent of pleasure into married Sarah. She moaned and said I love when a man ejaculates his warm sperm inside my vagina, feels so fucking good. She turned around and kissed me as we held each other and fell to the bed.

Sarah said oh yeah, I finally got some black in me. I said my pleasure to break you in love. She said don't worry Steve knows that I was going to fuck you. I said wow really, Sarah said Steve allows me to satisfy my black cravings with black men he approves of and he definitely approves of you. I said that is great to hear.

Sarah said I hope you don't mind that Steve fucked me in your man cave last night. I said I don't mind. Sarah kissed me and said you are the coolest neighbor ever. I said you have the perfect body. Sarah turned bright red from the compliment. We slept naked cuddle up smiling at each other after wonderful coitus.

I woke up with a warm sensation on my cock curtesy of hot Sarah. I smiled and said good morning, Sarah, she replied, good morning my sexy chocolate lover.

She laid down and said fuck me and don't stop until you ejaculate. I said yes goddess. She giggled, I kissed her penetrating her deep. I fucked her slowly then picked it up.

Shelby walked in and said are you two done fucking yet I'm hungry. Sarah said as soon as we are done, I'll make you breakfast. I fucked Sarah harder with no mercy as her daughter watched, Sarah moaned oh god here it comes as she moisturized my cock with her cream. I followed moments later ejaculating my warm sperm inside her horny cunt.

I kissed Sarah and she held me tight. I pulled out of Sarah with her daughter watching then Sarah said I'll go make us all breakfast in your fancy kitchen. Shelby looked at my cock, kissed me on the lips and said good morning stud then left. I watched her sexy ass jiggle away in the sexiest of manner.

We sat down to eat; Shelby scarfed down her breakfast then went swimming. I said does she know that her dad approves of us fucking. Sarah said she knows, I said cool, I'm glad that she knows the situation.

Two weeks of fucking and sucking with Sarah went by quick as shit. Steve came back on a Saturday morning. I went to pick him up, first thing, he asked how are my girls? I said they are great. Sarah was happy to see her husband and Shelby was happy to see her dad.

Sarah asked if we could watch a movie in my home theatre. I said sure and I set it up, I gave her a selection of movies. She chose a movie with a lot of sex scenes in it.

Sarah and Steve watched in the front row, while Shelby and I watched 5 rows back. Shelby held my hand and kissed me during one of the sex scenes. I was hard as shit with Shelby wearing the shortest dress possible showing off her sweet white thighs.

We both watched as Sarah put her head in Steve's lap and started bobbing up and down. Shelby took that opportunity to take my dick out and started sucking me with her wonderful mouth up and down.

I enjoyed it a lot, her mom smiled at me as Shelby sucked my cock. Sarah slid down Steve's white pole and started moaning loudly. Shelby held my black pole and slid her nineteen-year-old tight white pussy down my black pole. I couldn't believe that my 44-year-old cock was deep inside a hot 19-year-old college babe.

I took her big tits out and sucked the hell out of them as she fucked my cock with reckless abandon. I heard Sarah scream as she creamed Steve's cock then Shelby creamed my cock with a big scream. Moments later, Steve ejaculated inside of Sarah with a large grunt. I moaned as I ejaculated inside of Shelby for the first time, damn it was hot and intense as shit.

Sarah yelled did you enjoy my daughters 19-year-old vagina. I said oh yeah, it was amazing to fuck her tight 19-year-old vagina and she ask Shelby if she liked her first big black penis. She said oh yeah mom, I love being penetrated by my first big black pole.

**The end**